The Unbeatable Bread

Lyn Littlefield Hoopes

Pictures by *Brad Sneed*

Dial Books for Young Readers
 New York

 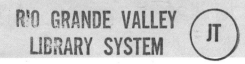

Published by Dial Books for Young Readers
A Division of Penguin Books USA Inc.
375 Hudson Street
New York, New York 10014

Designed by Nancy R. Leo
Printed in Hong Kong
First Edition
10 9 8 7 6 5 4 3 2 1

Library of Congress Cataloging in Publication Data
Hoopes, Lyn Littlefield.
The unbeatable bread / by Lyn Littlefield Hoopes ; pictures by Brad Sneed.
p.   cm.
Summary: The aroma of a special bread subdues the effects of a harsh
winter and draws people and animals to unite in a fabulous feast.
ISBN 0-8037-1611-7 (trade).—ISBN 0-8037-1612-5 (lib.)
[1. Bread—Fiction. 2. Stories in rhyme.]
I. Sneed, Brad, ill. II. Title.
PZ8.3.H77Un 1996   [E]—dc20   94-17043   CIP   AC

The paintings were done with oils on gessoed watercolor paper.

For Uncle Jon and Michelle, and for Liza, with love—L.L.H.

For Delores—B.S.

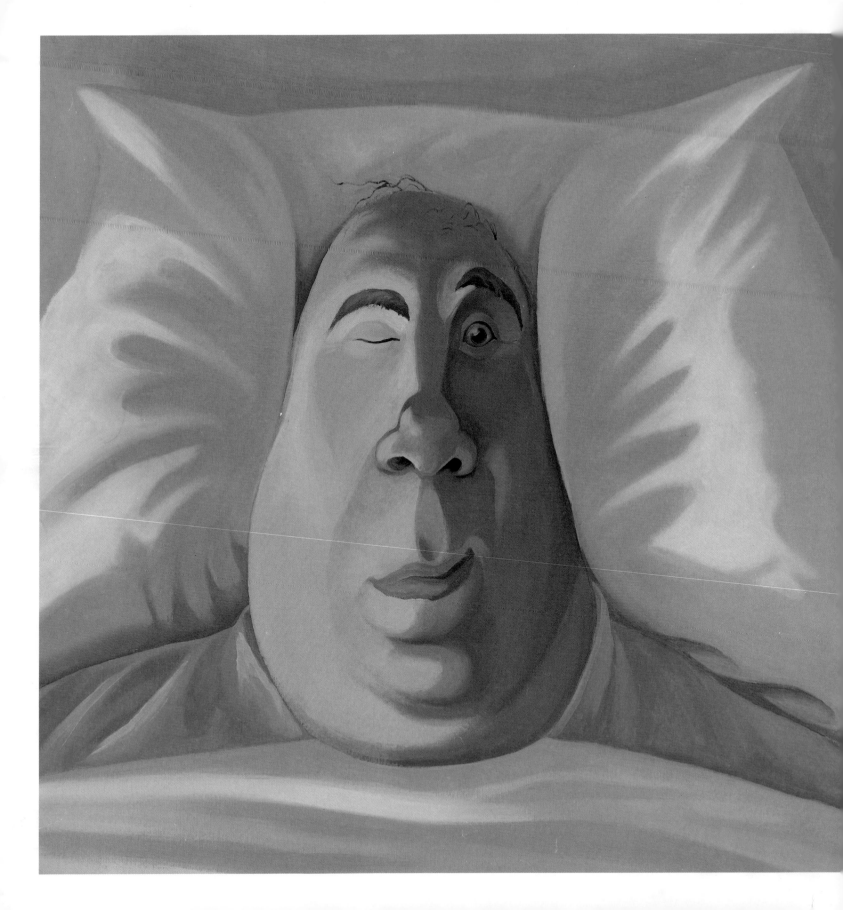

One dark morning
still dreaming in bed,
Uncle Jon sat up and said,
"I will bake an unbeatable bread."

"Bread?" sighed Aunt Lucy. "Oh, dread!"

"A wild bread," said Uncle Jon.
"A wishing bread
as bright as dawn…"

His wife gave a tremendous yawn.

"Uncle Jon,
  the children are grown.
  We've no one to eat it,
  no nieces or nephews or cousins to knead it!
  No grammas, no grampas,
  no good great-aunts…"

Uncle Jon pulled on his pants.

"I will bake an unbeatable bread.
  I'll wake the world from winter's sleep,
  melt the snow, the dark so deep;
  I'll break the spell of this long freeze,
  bring out the children and the honeybees."

Aunt Lucy gave a substantial sneeze.

"Uncle Jon, you've baked enough.
 The kitchen is full of poofs and puffs,
 cookies and crumb cakes with chocolatey chips…"

Uncle Jon just licked his lips.

"I will bake an unbeatable bread,
 an undefeatable bread!
 A YES bread, make-a-mess bread,
 a LOUD bread, feed-a-crowd bread…"

Aunt Lucy sat straight up and said,
"Mr. Makin' Bread, Mr. Muffin Head,
if we've no one to eat it,
and we're snowed in tight,
you'll be the one to eat every last bite.
Now stop your bakin',
pack up your pans,
stop eatin' the dough
off of your hands,
stop clanging your spoons,
singing your songs,
banging about with your bing bang bongs…"

"I'm bakin' a bread,"
  sang Uncle Jon,
"a wakin' bread.
  I'm bakin' a shakin' wakin' bread."

Aunt Lucy pulled the pillow over her head.
She knew there'd be no one
to eat that bread.

Uncle skipped to the kitchen
stuffed with poofs and puffs,
pulled out the bread pans
and all the bread stuffs,
and as he worked,
he hummed along,
singing his wakin' bakin' song.

"I'm bakin' a bread,
  a wakin' bread,
  bakin' a shakin' wakin' bread."

He mixed in the yellow
of the morning sun,
a whistle in the wind,
clouds on the run.

The bread dough rose
as he sang along.
He rolled it in a loaf,
and it wasn't long
'til the smell of bread baking
rose up with his song.

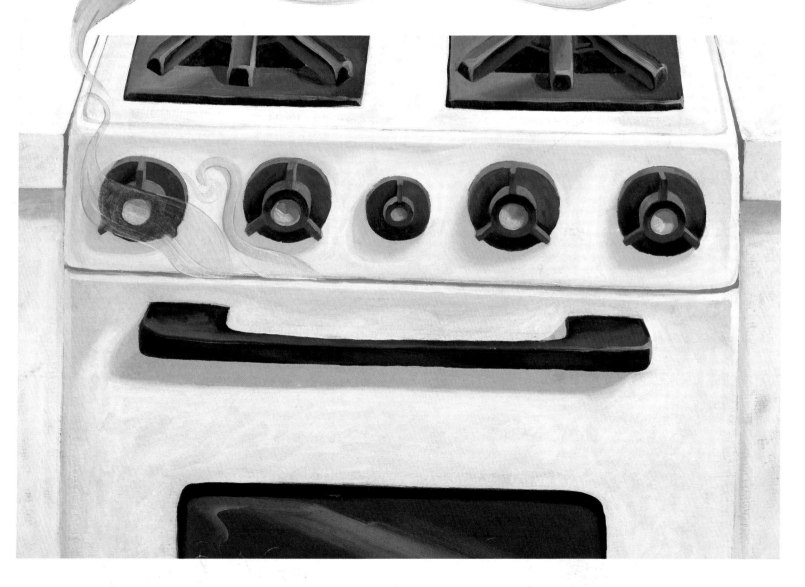

It floated upstairs
and along the halls,
slid out the iced windows
through cold, damp walls.
It sailed over trees all robed in white,
wrapped 'round the houses
snowed in tight.

The sweet wheaty smell
seeped under doors,
rose softly ringing
through cracks in floors.

It floated by firesides
in sleepy dogs' yawns,
played in fiddles
and old French horns,
slipped into hats,
mufflers, and mittens,
wrapped around alley cats
and little skinny kittens.

Now, alone by the window
Uncle watched the snow,
blowing deep, drifting slow;
and as he watched, he hummed along,
whispered his wakin' bakin' song.

"I'm bakin' a bread,
a wakin' bread,
bakin' a shakin' wakin' bread."

The sweet smell roamed
over snowy billows
and great white hills
like giant pillows.
It blew into bear caves
and foxes' dens,
woke rabbits and moles
and sleeping wrens.

It whispered 'round snowmen
stooped under trees,
and whistled in hives of honeybees,
rose into bedrooms,
rumbled in snores,
and crept with the spiders over nursery doors.

"A wakin' bread,
a shakin' bread,
bakin' a shakin' wakin' bread…"
Uncle scrubbed up as he sang along,
and the smell of bread baking
sailed on with his song.

It floated over bumps
and little lump-lumps;
it pooled in quilts,
and climbed mountainous rumps.

Then silently, secretly by it slid,
and found them each
under pillows hid.
Emma and Mia,
Liza, Sam, Miss Boo,
on it went to find Stevie too.

OFF with the blankets!
OFF-OFF with the spreads!
OFF with the sheets
on the winter white beds!

The smell of bread
reached down deep,
lifted them each out of sleep,
and waking them
with dreams of spring,
it wafted them off on great soft wings.

The sea sang silver,
and the skinny moon smiled
as they sailed away the morning miles,
and the gray sky ran to gold and red
with the perfect browning of the bread.

Now here was the sun,
up and coming,
and here was Stevie,
hum-hum-humming.
And a tap on the window,
two, three, four,
Emma and Mia
rapping on the door.

"Makin' a bread,
  a bread so fine…"
  Uncle Jon sang in the big sunshine.

"Bakin' a bread,
  a bread so true!"
  There was Liza and Sam and old Miss Boo.

"Bakin' a bread,
  a bread so proud!"
  Up flew the bees in a soft brown cloud.

"Bakin' a bread,
  a bread so good!"

  In came the creatures
  from the wood,
  rabbits and moles
  and singing wrens,
  foxes and bears hungry from their dens.

"Bakin' a bread,
 an undefeatable bread!"
Aunt Lucy woke to the sun overhead,
 popped off her pillow to smell that bread.

"Bakin' a bread,
 an *unbeatable* bread!"
Aunt Lucy tiptoed out of bed,
 and snuck downstairs to see that bread.

Uncle Jon swung wide the kitchen door,
 and in they came, dripping on the floor,
 gathered 'round and ready, waiting to be fed

a great big bite of the unbeatable bread.